Nice Try, Tooth Fairy

Nice Try, Tooth Fairy

By Mary W. Olson

Illustrated by Katherine Tillotson

SCHOLASTIC INC.
New York Toronto London Auckland Sydney
Mexico City New Delhi Hong Kong Buenos Aires

ISBN0-439-28817-7

12 11 10 9 8 7 6 5 4 3 2   2 3 4 5 6 7/0

Printed in the U.S.A.   08

First Scholastic printing, January 2002

Book design by Lily Malcolm
The text for this book is set in Lemonade.
The illustrations are rendered in oil.

To my husband, Doug, and my
two boys, Eric and Michael,
for all their love and support
—M. W. O.

To my parents,
Henry and Elizabeth
—K. T.

Dear Tooth Fairy,
 My mother says I should be pleased that you think I have such big teeth. But I think you made a mistake. Please can I have _my_ tooth back?

Emma

Dear Tooth Fairy,
    No, my tooth isn't this small, either. I almost didn't see it under my pillow. Just as I was about to pick it up, a funny-looking creature tumbled through my window and grabbed it. I guess it was his.

                    Emma

Dear Tooth Fairy,
        You sure must have a lot of teeth there. My mother says the tooth you left me last night is an alligator tooth. I'm looking for a place to put it so he'll be sure to find it!
        Here's a picture of my tooth, in case you forgot what it looked like.
                                Emma